READ ALONE

Get set with Read Alone!

This entertaining series is designed for all new readers who want to start reading a whole book on their own.

The stories are lively and fun, with lots of illustrations and clear, large type, to make first solo reading a perfect pleasure!

Other titles in the series

Jan Mark

The Twig Thing

Illustrated by Sally Holmes

VIKING

VIKING

Published by the Penguin Group
27 Wrights Lane, London W8 5TZ, England
Viking Penguin Inc., 40 West 23rd Street, New York, New York 10010, USA
Penguin Books Australia Ltd, Ringwood, Victoria, Australia
Penguin Books Canada Ltd, 2801 John Street, Markham, Ontario, Canada L3R 1B4
Penguin Books (NZ) Ltd, 182-190 Wairau Road, Auckland 10, New Zealand

Penguin Books Ltd, Registered Offices: Harmondsworth, Middlesex, England

First published 1988
10 9 8 7 6 5 4 3 2

Copyright © Jan Mark, 1988
Illustrations copyright © Sally Holmes, 1988

Printed in Great Britain by Butler & Tanner Ltd, Frome, Somerset

British Library Cataloguing in Publication Data

Mark, Jan
The twig thing. — (Read alone).
I. Title   II. Series
823'.914[J] PZ7

ISBN 0-670-82145-4

For Rosie and Ella

Contents

Upstairs and Upstairs

As soon as Rosie and
Ella saw the house they
knew that something was
missing. The house was tall
and thin. It stood on the
pavement.

Rosie said, "Where is the garden?"

"Gardens are at the back," Ella said.

"It's got a lot of windows," Daddy said.

They stood in the street and counted: one door and seven windows.

There was no garden at the front of the house, only a paved place for the dustbin and three steps up to the door. The top step was where a milk bottle lived. It looked as if it had lived there for a long time.

"Let's go in," said
Daddy. "It's our house
now."

Inside was a hall, a
kitchen and a dining-room.

Rosie said, "Where's the
garden?"

"Gardens are at the
back," Ella said.

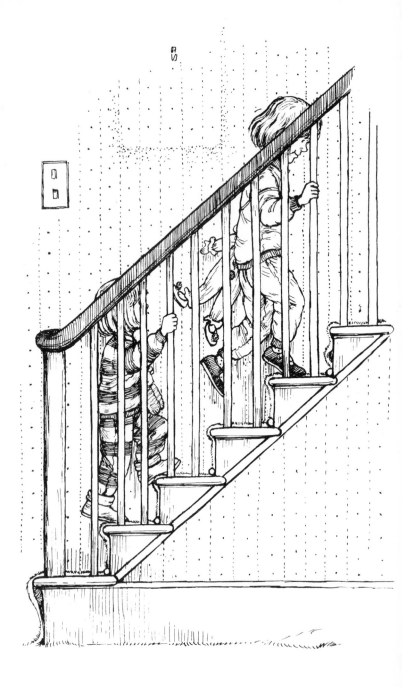

So they looked out of the window in the dining-room, but there was no garden at the back, only a long drop to the ground.

"There is a garage underneath," Daddy said. "Come upstairs."

Upstairs was a big living-room and two small rooms.

"This room is Ella's," said Daddy, and he opened the door of the first small room.

"This one is Rosie's," he said, and he opened the door of the next room. It was even smaller.

Ella said, "Where's the garden?"

Rosie said, "Gardens are at the back," because Ella had said that gardens are at the back. So they looked out of the living-room window, but there was only a very long drop to the ground, and no garden.

"Come upstairs," Daddy
said.

Rosie said, "More
upstairs?"

Ella said, "In our last
house you could only go
upstairs once."

"There must be a garden somewhere," Rosie said.

"There is a garden," said Daddy.

They went upstairs again. There was one big bedroom and one very big bedroom and a bathroom.

20

"This room is for visitors," Daddy said, and he opened the door of the big bedroom at the front. Then he opened the door of the very big bedroom at the back. "And this one is for me," he said.

Ella said, "It's too big for only you."

"For me and my books," said Daddy.

Rosie said, "Where's the garden?" They looked out of the window of Daddy's bedroom because it was at the back. There was no garden, only a terribly long drop to the ground.

Rosie said, "This is a very dangerous house."

22

23

"Come upstairs," said
Daddy.

Ella said, "More
upstairs? These stairs only
go into the ceiling."

Daddy said, "No, they
don't. Look again," and he
pointed.

At the top of the stairs
was a door. It was lying on
its back in the middle of the
ceiling. Daddy went up the

stairs and opened the door.
Rosie and Ella climbed
behind him. They looked
up and saw the sky.

26

"Here you are," Daddy
said. "This is the garden."
They looked round and
saw the garden.
It was on the roof.

Sky High

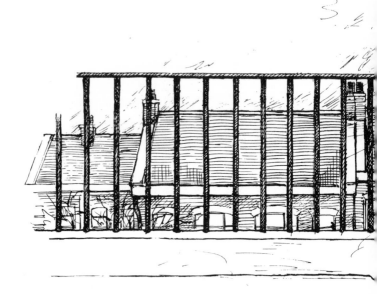

Rosie said, "This isn't a garden, it's a pavement."

Ella said, "It is a garden. There are plant pots."

"There are no plants," said Rosie.

28

29

"Stay away from the railings," Daddy said, so they went to the railings. Ella went to the front railing and Rosie went to the one at the back. On both sides there was a fearfully long drop to the ground.

Rosie said, "This is the most dangerous house I have ever lived in."

Ella said, "I wish I could fly."

Daddy said, "Don't try.
You must never come up
here without me."

"I don't ever want to
come up here," Rosie said.
"I want to go back to the
other house and play on

the grass. There isn't any
grass here. It's cold and
windy and it's not a real
garden."

"It will be," Daddy said. "We will make it into a real garden in the spring. It won't be cold and windy then."

Ella said, "It won't be

spring for ages. Can we
have tea?"

So they went downstairs,
and downstairs again, and
down some more stairs,
until they found the
kitchen.

But all the mugs and plates were in boxes and they could not find the teapot. Daddy made tea in the milk jug and they drank it out of eggcups.

There was only one chair. Daddy sat on the chair. Ella sat on his right knee and Rosie sat on his left knee and they all ate sandwiches.

"Tomorrow the furniture will come," Daddy said.

Ella said, "But where shall we sleep tonight?"

"You two can sleep in my bed," Daddy said. "It's already here."

Rosie said, "Where will you sleep?"

"I shall hang upside-down from the ceiling," Daddy said. "Like a bat."

Ella helped Daddy to
wash up. Rosie went to the
front door because there
was something she wanted
to look at. In the front door
was another, very small,
front door.

Rosie said, "What is this
for?"

"That is a catflap,"
Daddy said.

Ella said, "We haven't
got a cat."

"Then we must get one,"
said Daddy. "We can't
have a catflap without a
cat."

Rosie opened the catflap and looked out into the dark street. It was still windy and cold. The wind blew across the top of the milk bottle and made it moan.

Rosie felt sorry for the milk bottle, all alone in the dark on the cold step. She fetched some crumbs from the kitchen and threw them out of the catflap, on to the top step, in case the poor milk bottle felt hungry in the night.

The wind blew litter
along the pavement.

A paper bag went past,
and a black feather, and
then a cardboard box. The
wind blew a twig thing

along the street and it stuck
behind the dustbin.

"Come to bed now," said
Daddy, so Ella and Rosie
went upstairs, and upstairs
again, to the bathroom.

Then they went
downstairs, once, and got
into Daddy's bed, which
was in the living-room for
now.

Daddy gave them a hug
and sang to them until they
went to sleep.

The Twig Thing

Next morning Rosie
woke up early and went
downstairs. In the dining-
room Daddy was asleep.

He was not hanging from
the ceiling, he was on the
floor in a sleeping bag.

Rosie went past very
quietly and opened the
catflap. Outside on the step

48

the milk bottle was still
there, but the crumbs had
gone.

And the twig thing was
still there, stuck behind the
dustbin. Rosie could see it

properly now. It had a
neck, and two front legs,
and two back legs, and a
long stiff tail, but it wasn't
an animal, it was a twig. It
looked cold.

Then Ella got up and
jumped on Daddy, so
Daddy got up too and they
had breakfast.

After that a van arrived
with all the furniture in it,
and two men carried the

furniture inside. Daddy helped them. While the front door was open Rosie slipped out to the dustbin and fetched the twig thing.

"Don't run off and get lost," said Daddy, when he saw her. So Rosie went and sat in the kitchen with Ella and watched the furniture go by.

When all the furniture was in, the men went away with the van.

"Lunch time," Daddy
said. He had been
unpacking, so for lunch
they had eggs in the
eggcups and made tea in
the teapot and drank it out
of mugs.

"What have you got
there?" Daddy said.

"This is my twig thing,"
Rosie said. "I found it by
the dustbin. It came last
night."

Daddy looked at it.
"Let's put it in water," he
said.

But they could not find a
vase.

"I know," said Ella, and went to the catflap. She put out her arm and brought in the milk bottle. Rosie filled it with water and put the twig thing in the water.

Daddy put the milk bottle on the window sill and the twig thing stood there on its tail, with its four legs stuck out and its neck in the air.

"It looks like an animal," Ella said. "A very thin animal with only bones and no fur."

"I shall call it Twiggy," Rosie said.

"Let's call it Puss," said Ella, "until we get a cat."

"I should call it May," said Daddy, "because I think that's what it will be."

So the twig thing stood on the window sill in the

kitchen. Rosie was glad
because it was warm now,
and the milk bottle was
warm too.

Every time she went into
the kitchen she said,

60

"Hello, May."

"I wish it could talk,"
Rosie said. "I wish it would
say, 'Hello, Rosie'."

"It's too busy growing to
talk," Daddy said.

61

"I'm growing," said Rosie, "and I can talk."

"But you aren't a twig thing," said Daddy. "You are my beautiful Rosie."

"What about me?" said Ella.

"You are my lovely Ella and you are growing too," Daddy said.

"The twig thing grows faster than us," said Rosie.

"If you didn't talk so much," said Daddy, "you might grow faster too."

The Tree

After a while Ella went
to her new school. Rosie
went to playgroup in the
morning and in the

afternoon she went to a
lady down the road who
looked after children.
Daddy went to work.

In the evening they all came home and had tea together.

They got a cat. It was a thin little cat and they

called it Twiggy. Twiggy
went in and out of the
catflap, out in the morning,
back again at night.
Daddy said that she was
going to work too.

On the kitchen window sill the twig thing stood in the milk bottle. It was getting bigger. At the end of its legs grew little green buds, like paws. At the end of its neck was a much bigger bud, like a head.

Twiggy was growing bigger too. Sometimes she brought home a mouse. That was Twiggy's work, catching mice.

Outside in the street the wind stopped blowing and the sun shone. It shone into the kitchen window and the buds on the twig thing opened. They were leaves. More leaves grew along its legs, like green fur.

One day Rosie went into the kitchen and said, "Hello, May."

"Look at its head," said Daddy, and he pointed. The twig thing's head was covered in small white flowers.

"I said it would be May,"
Daddy told her.

The sun went on shining.

"Can we go into the
garden yet?" Ella said.

"I think we can now,"
Daddy said, so they all
went upstairs, upstairs and

upstairs, to the roof.
Twiggy came too.

They counted the plant
pots.

"Six," said Rosie.

"Seven," said Ella, who
went to school. "We must
buy some seeds."

"We must buy some earth," Daddy said, and next day he brought home a bagful. Rosie had never seen earth in a bag, before. It was called Potting Compost.

Rosie said, "Where are the seeds?"

"We will all go out tomorrow and choose them," Daddy said.

"I want to plant something now," said Rosie.

"Then we shall," Daddy

said. "Come on up to the roof."

So they all went up to the roof with Twiggy. Daddy opened the bag and put

some earth into the biggest
plant pot.

"Now fetch your twig
thing," said Daddy to
Rosie, and she went
downstairs, downstairs and
downstairs to the kitchen.

The twig thing stood in
its milk bottle on the
kitchen window sill. The

flowers had died but the
leaves were green and
strong. Rosie lifted it down
and carried it up to the
roof.

Daddy said, "Now, put it

in the plant pot," and Rosie
did it. The twig thing stood
in its new pot and looked
like a little green tree.

"It may grow into a real
tree," said Daddy, "if we
hope very hard and treat it
kindly."

So they all stood round the twig thing in its pot, and held hands and hoped very hard.

It was the first plant in the garden.